Handy Stories
to Read and Sign

Donna Jo Napoli and Doreen DeLuca

Illustrated by Maureen Klusza

Gallaudet University Press
Washington, DC

Gallaudet University Press
Washington, DC 20002
http://gupress.gallaudet.edu

Printed in Korea

Library of Congress Cataloging-in-Publication Data

Napoli, Donna Jo, 1948-
   Handy stories to read and sign / Donna Jo Napoli and Doreen DeLuca ;
   illustrated by Maureen Klusza.
       p. cm.
   ISBN 978-1-56368-407-4 (alk. paper)
   1. Sign language--Juvenile literature. 2. Children's stories, American. I. DeLuca,
   Doreen. II. Klusza, Maureen, ill. III. Title.
   HV2476.N37 2009
   419'.7086--dc22   2009012624

Contents

Authors' Note

Dear Parents and Teachers,

The stories in this book are written for beginning readers. They are fun to read in both English and American Sign Language (ASL). The signs are made by a right-handed signer, so if you are left-handed, just reverse the movements you see on the page.

Each of the five stories takes place in a different month of the year, September through January, which helps children build on real-life experiences. The stories increase in complexity as the child's vocabulary and reading skills increase during the school year. The first story, for example, is told entirely in single-word sentences, while the last story contains several complete sentences. A new reader can, therefore, focus on the act of reading and on building recognition skills before having to learn how written English is different from ASL or any other language. In this way, the stories are organized to welcome all new readers of English, regardless of their native language.

In the first three stories, the ASL signs appear directly under the corresponding English words. However, English and ASL have quite different sentence structures. As a result, there is not a word-for-sign match between ASL and English. In the fourth and fifth stories, which include whole sentences, the ASL signs are sometimes placed on a different part of the page from the English sentences so readers do not become confused.

Please note that the sign drawings are not a writing system. In sign languages the hands, arms, head, face, and torso work hard (they lean, shake, take on a certain form, etc.), so no simple writing system would be adequate to represent them.

We hope you and your children enjoy these stories. Happy reading!

Donna Jo Napoli and Doreen DeLuca

School Signs

Children develop many strategies in learning to read. One of the earliest strategies is memorization. Children simply memorize a story and, eventually, they learn to match the words they hear, or the signs they see, with the words printed on the page. Rhyme and rhythm are factors that aid memorization, and these are the factors that move "School Signs" along.

Each set of facing pages in this story contains a rhyme in English; just look at the final words—*bump/jump* and *three/C* —for example. The last page repeats the words on the first page.

The concept of rhyme in ASL may be new to the reader. Every sign consists of at least four parameters or parts: a handshape, a location, a movement, and an orientation (which way the palm faces). As an example, let's look at the very first sign of the book, RIDE:

1. **handshape:** The right hand is a Bent V. The left hand is a C.
2. **location:** The hands are in front of the body.
3. **movement:** The Bent V fingers of the right hand hook onto the thumb of the left hand, and both hands move forward.
4. **orientation:** The right palm faces down and the left palm faces right.

When signs have parameters in common, they rhyme. The more parameters they have in common, the stronger the rhyme. In this story, there are many rhymes, from strong ones like SCHOOL/JUMP and JUMP/DANCE, to medium ones like RIDE/JUMP and TRAIN/MUSIC, to light ones like 3/BUMP and A/DRUM.

The rhythm in both ASL and English is 1-and-a-2. Have fun bumping through this story!

Ride.

Bump! Bump! Bump!

School.

Jump! Jump! Jump!

Friends.

1　　2　　3

Train.

A B C

Cookie.

Yum! Yum! Yum!

Music.

Drum! Drum! Drum!

Dance.   **F-E-E-T**   **Hands.**   **Head.**

 **Colors.**  **Blue.**  **Green.**  **Red.**

Time.

Jump! Jump! Jump!

Ride.

Bump! Bump! Bump!

Haunted House

Like our first story, this second story is easy to memorize. However, while "School Signs" had many rhymes in both English and ASL, "Haunted House" contains several rhymes in ASL but not in English.

The rhythm is strong in both languages and it carries the story, allowing the child a better chance at memorization. The rhythm is very simple: AAA, BBB, CDE, where A is a given word/sign, B is another word/sign, and C, D, and E are all different words/signs. This pattern happens four times. The final page has just one word/sign on it—the big surprise ending.

This story also highlights a difference between ASL and English. ASL uses classifier signs to characterize certain shapes, sizes, and objects. While our first story used only one classifier—the handshape for BUMP, which represents vehicles—this story uses classifiers repeatedly to form sentence predicates. For example, the upside-down Bent V represents the girl as she climbs up the steps; the 1 handshape represents the girl backing up and later smacking into the mirror. This story also uses a classifier to indicate the mirror in the sign SMACK.

We encourage teachers to point out that two different classifiers are used for the girl in this story, depending on how we want to show her moving. Teachers can also explain that classifiers represent the shape and size of an object, as well as the type of object. For example, if the story were about a cat instead of a girl, the classifier for the cat backing up would be different from the classifier for the girl, but the English words would stay the same. In other words, ASL, through the use of classifiers, packs more information into its predicates than English does.

This difference between ASL and English is fundamental to understanding the grammatical contrasts between the two languages. The child who uses ASL needs to understand it early in the learning-to-read process.

"Haunted House" pays tribute to a famous ABC classifier story by the same name. ABC stories use all the handshapes of the alphabet in sequence, whether forward, backward, or both. We hope this allusion to ASL literature will stimulate the reader's appetite for more.

Onward to the surprise!

 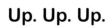 Up. Up. Up.

 Knock! Knock! Knock!

 Open.

 Dark.

 Nothing.

Look! Look! Look!

There! There! There!

Spider.   **Bat.**   **Frog.**

No! No! No!

Back! Back! Back!

Witch.

Ghost.

Vampire.

Run! Run! Run!

Pound! Pound! Pound!

Smack!

Who?

Ah!

Me!

Thanksgiving Soon

This story is also easy to memorize, and it includes several ASL rhymes. In both languages, the rhythm is strong and regular. We have also added a new device here—the refrain—that helps readers to see how the story is divided into different sections.

Each section uses the pattern form ABC followed by a brief comment and the refrain of "Thanksgiving soon." A, B, and C are always syntactically uniform and the comment is a single word/sign. There are only two exceptions. The first occurs when the turkey tries his first solution: "Hide!" precedes the pattern on that page. The second is found on the next-to-last page, when the turkey finds his real solution. Here, "Got it!" precedes the final pattern.

In most cases, A, B, and C are single or compound words/signs. However, in two instances, they are propositions (meaningful units that usually correspond to a sentence). "Chickens eat" is a proposition; it tells us that the chickens are eating, and it is a sentence in both English and ASL.

In this story, readers see full sentences for the first time. Sentences present a new complication for them because English and ASL have different rules about what must be present in a sentence. An English sentence requires a verb, but an ASL sentence can consist of a noun plus any other word type that assigns a property to (or gives information about) that noun, with or without a verb present. For example, LUCKY FARMERS is a proposition that tells us the farmers are lucky. In English, this unit does not form a sentence, while in ASL it does. Yet in both languages, the semantic proposition is clear. Similarly, THANKSGIVING SOON, is a sentence in ASL, not in English, but in both languages it is a proposition. This story offers the teacher or parent a chance to discuss with the child an important difference in the syntactic structures of the two languages.

Finally, we have introduced a lexical issue that any bilingual text must face. Languages do not carve out the world in the same way. One language will use a given word for only one function, while another language will use its counterpart for many functions. English and ASL have many lexical mismatches of this type. In "Thanksgiving Soon" the English word *eat* corresponds to three different signs in ASL: one sign to show how chickens eat, one sign to show how cows eat, and one sign to show how farmers eat. Children whose first language is ASL need to be alerted to lexical mismatches and become accustomed to memorizing them.

Wind.

Cold.

Leaves.

Autumn.

Thanksgiving soon.

Apples.

Corn.

Nuts.

Yum!

Thanksgiving soon.

Chickens eat.

Cows eat.

Farmers eat.

Oops!

Thanksgiving soon.

Pumpkins.

Potatoes

Turkeys.

Yikes!

Thanksgiving soon.

Lucky farmers.

Lucky cows.

Lucky chickens.

Hide!   Tree?   Water?   Hole?

What now?   Thanksgiving soon.

Got it!

Scarf.　　　　Pants.　　　　Hat.

Safe!　　　　Thanksgiving soon.

Winter Solstice

Now we move to another level of difficulty. As always, our eye is on the job of memorization as the means of identifying words. To that end, "Winter Solstice" is rich with rhyme in ASL, and it includes much repetition. It also has an intermittent refrain in the form of "X, X all around," where X is a single word. In fact, this story can be considered a prose poem.

Unlike the previous stories, this one is told primarily in sentences. The ideas are straightforward and supported by the illustrations. The sentences have simple structure, but the readers' task is enormous because English and ASL are so different syntactically. We tackle several such differences in "Winter Solstice."

Here, children repeatedly see English sentences that contain a form of the verb *be*, a verb that has no counterpart in ASL. Additionally, we introduce the English article *the*, which is not rendered by any sign in ASL. Readers also learn that, unlike ASL, English indicates past time with changes in the verb form, whether or not a time adverbial (such as *yesterday*) is present.

Children also will see a new kind of lexical mismatch in this story. For example, the English word *away* appears twice, once in "fly away" and once in "jump away." While English simply adds *away* after the verb, ASL incorporates the notion into the predicate verb. This is an important difference between English and ASL; relational notions (whether spatial or temporal) are often indicated by prepositions in English and by changes in the predicate in ASL.

Finally, we need to mention here not just what we have included in this story, but what we have left out. The English sentences in "Winter Solstice" are printed in the middle of each page, below the illustrations. For the first time, children must concentrate on reading the words to understand the story. The ASL propositions, in contrast, are placed lower on the page, without any translations. We did this to show the children that, most of the time, ASL cannot be translated sign-for-word into English due to the different syntactic structures of these two languages.

Yesterday the ground was warm. Today
the ground is white. Snow, snow, all around.

Nuts - squirrels hide them. Nuts - squrriels steal them.
Cold, cold, all around.

Children play. Children fall. Were there angels here?

Winter starts today.

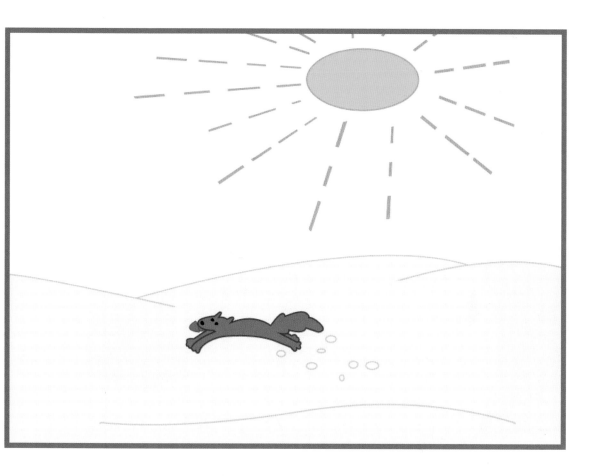

Snow under sun.

Birds gather. Birds fly away.
Dark, dark, all around.

Deer get scared. Deer jump away.
Stars, stars, all around.

Children sleep. Children dream. Winter starts tonight.

Snow under moon.

Class Pet

Ease of memorization has been our guiding principle all along, and it remains so in this final story. The ASL sentences have lots of rhyme, and both the English and ASL sentences repeat lexical items and syntactic structures.

As in our first three stories, most of the sign drawings in "Class Pet" are right beside the English words. But unlike our first three stories, there is no simple correlation between individual words and individual signs. After the fourth story, readers should realize that one-to-one correspondence between English and ASL sentences is rarely possible. The languages are far too different for that. So here, the sign drawings create grammatically correct ASL sentences; they are not sign-for-word translations of the English sentences. We put the English words and the ASL signs side by side in order to make it clear who is talking without cluttering the illustrations.

Knowing who is talking is very important because this story is told in dialogue. It is meant to encourage role-playing, another activity that aids memorization. "Class Pet" has three speaking characters—a boy, a girl, and a storeowner. We encourage you to have the students act out this story. Treat it like a play and have fun.

A store.

What kind?

Animals.

Our class could use a pet.

Let's go in!

Pick one.

Help me.

A mouse.

Oops!

Catch it!

Where is it?

A snake.

Oops!

Catch it.

Where is it?

A cat.

Oops!

Again? Catch it.

Where is it?

The cat chases the snake. The snake chases the mouse.

The mouse chases...

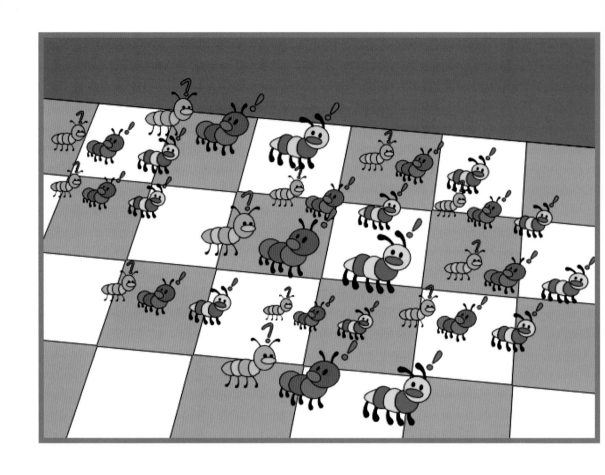

... bugs? Bugs!

Ugh!

The mouse eats the bugs.
The snake eats the bugs.
The cat eats the bugs.

Catch it, catch it, catch it. Yay!

Do you want a fish?

Why?

It can't escape.

53

How much?

For you? Free.

Why?

The bugs are gone. Thanks.